The Goose That Almost Got Cooked

The Goose That Almost Got Cooked

Story and Pictures by Marc Simont

SCHOLASTIC INC.
New York Toronto London Auckland Sydney
Mexico City New Delhi Hong Kong Buenos Aires

ISBN 0-439-24399-8

12 11 10 9 8 7 6 5 4 3 2 1 1 2 3 4 5 6/0

Printed in the U.S.A. 14

First Scholastic paperback printing, November 2001

The illustrations in this book are watercolor painting.
The text type is set in Caxton Book.
Book design by David Saylor

To Jane, Mary Margaret, and Sarah

When Emily was just a gosling swimming behind her mother, she loved to drop out of line to swim around in little circles.

As a grown-up goose, Emily was still dropping out of line — only now it was to do flips and loop-the-loops.

"You'll get tired doing that," said her friend Sam.

But Emily ignored him — for she always liked to do as she pleased.

It was a long flight to Lake Artok, where the flock spent summers, so Emily amused herself by doing flips. Just as Sam had warned, she soon grew so tired, she couldn't keep up. Completely exhausted, Emily glided to the ground. She tucked her head under a wing and fell asleep.

The next morning, Emily awoke to find seven large white geese standing over her. Before she could say hello, they turned and waddled away to where a farmer was serving breakfast. Emily followed and had a delicious meal of corn, wheat, and celery tops.

When the sun went down, the farmer walked the geese over to a little shed where they would be safe from foxes and raccoons. When the farmer saw Emily, his face lit up with a smile.

To Emily, this seemed like an ideal life.

"I think I'll stay here," she decided.

As time went on, Emily settled contentedly into the easy life of the farm. It all seemed perfect until. . .

. . . one morning, when Emily sensed that something was wrong. She looked at her companions, sleeping soundly in the familiar shed. There should have been seven white geese. Now Emily counted only six!

Emily ate breakfast quickly, eager to find the missing goose. She searched all day long.

She was about to give up when she noticed a pail of white goose feathers. Emily's heart beat rapidly.

“Horrors!” Emily cried.

Now she understood why the farmer served such good breakfasts and why he kept foxes and raccoons from eating the geese. He wanted to eat them himself!

“I’m getting out of here,” Emily said. She ran as fast as she could, furiously flapping her wings for takeoff. But something was wrong. She wasn’t getting off the ground.

Emily had forgotten that this was the season when Canada geese lose their flight feathers. Emily was molting. She would have to wait for new feathers to grow before she could fly away.

Emily felt helpless and alone. For the first time since she had come to the farm, she thought about Sam and the rest of her flock. Would she ever see them again?

Emily's life was in danger. While anxiously waiting for new feathers to grow, Emily kept a watchful eye on the farmer and his wife. A week passed, then another.

Then one fateful day, the farmer's wife said, "Let's have the Canada goose for dinner."

She went to the little shed and let the geese out, one by one, until only Emily remained.

"Here, goosie, goosie," she said.

Poor Emily was trapped.

In desperation, Emily lunged forward, flailing her strong wings, and knocked the woman off balance. Emily, seeing her chance, flew past the farmer's wife and out the open door.

Flew?

Yes, Emily's flight feathers had grown back. Honking loudly with joy, she soared to the sky and flew towards Lake Artok as fast as her wings could take her.

All alone, she fought strong winds and fierce thunderstorms. Long distances had been much easier when everyone flew together.

Early one morning, Sam saw a tiny black speck in the sky.

"There's Emily," he called.

Sam flew up to meet her, and they glided down to the lake together.

It felt great to be back with her friends. . .

. . . but when the rest of the flock would settle for the evening, Emily still liked to soar to the sky to do flips and loop-the-loops with Sam — just for fun.

Simont, Marc
The Goose that almost got cooked